This book belongs to:

_____

A catalogue record for this book is available from the British Library
Published by Ladybird Books Ltd
80 Strand London WC2R 0RL
A Penguin Company
8 10 9 7
© Ladybird Books Ltd MMVI. This edition MMVIII

ISBN: 978-1-84646-984-8
Printed in China

The Little Red Hen

Retold by Vera Southgate M.A., B.Com
with illustrations by David Kearney

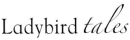

Ladybird *tales*

Once upon a time, there was a little red hen who lived in a farmyard.

One day the little red hen found some grains of wheat.

She took them to the other animals in the farmyard.

"Who will help me to plant these grains of wheat?" asked the little red hen.

"Not I," said the cat.

"Not I," said the rat.

"Not I," said the pig.

"Then I shall plant the grains myself," said the little red hen.

So she did.

Every day the little red hen went to the field to watch the grains of wheat growing.

They grew tall and strong.

One day, the little red hen saw that the wheat was ready to be cut.

"Now the wheat can be made into flour," said the little red hen to herself, as she set off for the farmyard.

"Who will help me to take the wheat to the mill, to be ground into flour?" asked the little red hen.

"Not I," said the cat.

"Not I," said the rat.

"Not I," said the pig.

"Then I shall take the wheat to the mill myself," said the little red hen.

So she did.

The little red hen took the wheat to the mill and the miller ground it into flour.

When the wheat had been ground into flour, the little red hen took it to the other animals in the farmyard.

"Who will help me to take this flour to the baker, to be made into bread?" asked the little red hen.

"Not I," said the cat.

"Not I," said the rat.

"Not I," said the pig.

"Then I shall take the flour to the baker myself," said the little red hen.

So she did.

The little red hen took the flour to the baker and the baker made it into bread.

When the bread was baked,
the little red hen took it to the
other animals in the farmyard.

"The bread is now ready to be eaten," said the little red hen. "Who will help me to eat the bread?"

"I will," said the cat.

"I will," said the rat.

"I will," said the pig.

"No, you will not," said the little red hen. "I shall eat it myself."

So she did.

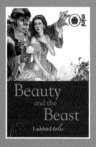

Beauty and the Beast
Ladybird tales

Cinderella
Ladybird tales

Hansel and Gretel
Ladybird tales

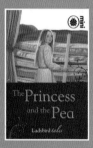

The Princess and the Pea
Ladybird tales

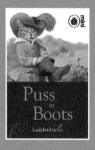

Puss in Boots
Ladybird tales

Sleeping Beauty
Ladybird tales

The Three Billy Goats Gruff
Ladybird tales

The Three Little Pigs
Ladybird tales

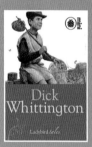

Dick Whittington
Ladybird tales

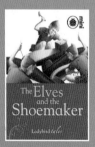

The Elves and the Shoemaker
Ladybird tales

The Little Red Hen
Ladybird tales

Snow White and the Seven Dwarfs
Ladybird tales